CW00847921

ISBN-13: 978-1539767084
ISBN-10: 1539767086

To Fabiana,

Thank you for your ongoing support, love and belief
regardless of scary moments

Love Nicky
xx

Acknowledgements

Books are such special things, they have a magical ability to bury into our hearts and souls, allowing us to learn about things, places and ourselves. My love of books has been one which spans years, and some of my favourites still sit on my book shelf. My dream to create my own books has been a long one, but it wasn't until I found my destination that they came to life, and even then they sat in my imagination for so long. I am delighted to be able to create the Adventures of Brian and bring the magic of books and the wonders of therapeutic storytelling together to offer a combination of stories and support to children and their families. Before we start this special story there is thanks to be given;

To my Mum and Dad, who have given me the encouragement to move forward with a dream of creating stories to help small people. Thank you for standing by me, encouraging me and sharing these precious moments.

To Richard for your belief and encouragement that there was a set of books inside me that should be written, this shiny diamond is very grateful.

To my nan and grandad, who forever guide me to follow this path that I am on and to ensure that I stay true to my dreams.

To Veronica, thank you for allowing me the privilege of naming Brian after Brian. There is a sprinkling of him all over each and every book I write.

To Fabiana, I could not ask for a better friend to set an example that even in scary moments we can find strength that we did not know existed. Thank you for your support and encouragement.

I hope you enjoy these books as much as I have enjoyed writing them

Love Nicky x x

THE ADVENTURES OF BRIAN

HELPING CHILDREN OVERCOME THEIR FEARS AND WORRIES

This book belongs to:

....

Brian had a scared feeling, he had woken up from his nap with the worried feeling in his tummy, Brian didn't like the worried feeling, it made him want his mummy!

He jumped out of his bed and hurried to find his mummy – but where was she? He couldn't find her anywhere.... He felt the worried feeling in his tummy and knew he had to find her....

He ran into the kitchen but she wasn't there, Brian didn't know where she was, he just wanted his mummy to make the feeling better......He checked in the cupboards and behind the tea towel but she wasn't hiding there......

So he ran to the bathroom, 'maybe she's in the bath' he thought – although he didn't know why she would choose to do that! He ran into the bathroom and looked all around, he put his paws on the edge of the bath and looked inside – she wasn't there either! 'Oh no' Brian thought!

'Hmm, maybe she is on the stairs?' he wondered. So he ran to the stairs, she wasn't on the stairs! 'Where is she?' he thought. He thought and thought…. He ran up the stairs but she wasn't up there either! "Mummy where are you?" he barked!

He climbed down the stairs carefully, just like mummy told him to and went into the living room, he jumped on the sofa, climbed behind the cushions, checked the fireplace and behind the curtains, she was nowhere to be found! "Mummy where are you?" he barked!

Then he heard a noise! He stopped….. and waited….. Where was it coming from? 'The garden!' he thought, how hadn't he noticed that the back door was open! Mummy was in the garden! Brian ran into the garden and there she was!

'Phew!' thought Brian and he felt the worried feeling getting smaller... He ran up to his mummy and jumped up to give her a cuddle. She scooped him up in her arms and gave him a big cuddle!

"You're awake! I missed you" mummy said!

Brian gave her a big lick!

"Did you worry that I had left you Brian?" She asked....

Brian licked her again and snuggled his head into her neck, resting his head on her shoulder for a big cuddle. "Oh Brian, I wouldn't leave you I love you too much!" she told him.

Brian was so happy that he had found his mummy, she carried him inside and he curled up on her lap and fell fast asleep....

That afternoon Mummy was in the kitchen so Brian went to play in the garden, he kept coming back to check she was still there "oh Brian I wouldn't leave you I love you too much!" she said when she noticed that he was checking.

Brian still felt a little bit scared though. He went to play outside with his ball. While he was outside his friend Blue Butterfly came fluttering down onto her flower.

Brian decided to tell Blue Butterfly about his scared feeling when he can't find his mummy.

Blue Butterfly explained "sometimes when we are feeling not like ourselves then it can leave us with a scared feeling and it makes us want to find the people we love to make us feel safe".

"But I don't like it, how can I make the funny feeling go away Blue Butterfly?" Brian asked.

Blue Butterfly looked at Brian and then she said, "You know when you go somewhere you love Brian?"

"Like the field with Boo?" Brian replied.

Blue Butterfly smiled, "Yes like the field with Boo – do you feel the worried feeling when you are with Boo Brian?"

Brian thought about the question for a moment, "No, I'm too happy to feel it then" he replied.

"Well when you are at home, or go out, or go to school wouldn't it be nice if you felt as happy as when you were with Boo?" Blue Butterfly asked.

"That would feel much better!" Brian said.

Blue Butterfly spread her wings and sat down on the flower, "When you feel happy what colour does it feel like in your tummy Brian?" she asked.

Brian thought about this for a moment..... "It's blue" he said! "Like your wings Blue Butterfly".

Blue Butterfly spread her wings and nodded again, "Well, the next time you are somewhere and the scared feeling starts I want you to close your eyes and think of something happy and that blue feeling. Then imagine the blue feeling flying all over your body to protect you and allow you to feel happy and brave".

Brian was a little bit quiet, "Can we practice, so I know how?" he asked.

"Of course we can!" Blue Butterfly replied, "Are you sitting comfortably?".

Brian sat down on the grass in front of the flower, "Yes I am!" Brian said smiling, he was very excited about letting the scared feeling go, his little tail started wiggling very, very fast!

"Ok, so close your eyes Brian, and I want you to find that lovely blue feeling that makes you feel happy and brave! Where in your body is it?" Blue Butterfly asked.

Brian tilted his head to the left, then he tilted his head to the right while he looked for the colour, "Yes it's in my tummy!" he said!

"Great, so I want you to let that blue feeling come to life, give it lots of energy, and let it start to fly all over your body, like magical shooting stars flying all around you and inside you! As they fly around the scared feeling is getting smaller and smaller and smaller" Blue Butterfly explained.

"Oooo" Brian wiggled on the spot, "It's moving very fast!".

"That's brilliant Brian, great, now shall we make that scared feeling disappear now?".

"Yes please!" Brian said!

"Well done Brian, ok, now it's time for the clever bit! I want you to make that blue feeling fly even FASTER! Those magical shooting stars will be flying all around you and inside you, and as they fly around faster and faster and faster the scared feeling is going get smaller and smaller!

Those shooting stars are moving even FASTER now! And that scared feeling is so small now you can barely find it! Are you ready Brian we need to push it out!" Blue Butterfly exclaimed!

Brian squeezed his eyes tight shut and wiggled with excitement, his tail was wiggling very fast now! His tummy felt full of happy, brave shooting stars now! "Ready!" he shouted!

"Brilliant Brian, ok, we need to push it right out now, so choose one of those shooting stars and I want you to use it to push that scared feeling out – Now, you can choose, you can push it out of your belly button, or your mouth or your ear, which one will you choose?".

"Ooo, my belly button!" Brian squealed, he was so excited!

"Ok Brian, those magical shooting stars are flying all around you and inside you. Quicker and quicker and as they fly around faster and faster and faster the scared feeling is getting so tiny now that you can barely see it and when I count to 5 it's going to just pop out of your belly button, and

the funny thing is, that it's so tiny you won't even feel it! Are you ready? Here we go!
1.....2......3.......4.........5!"

Brian giggled and as Blue Butterfly went quiet he slowly opened one eye and then the other…. He waited….. and then he waited a little bit longer….

The scared feeling was gone!

He ran round in a circle waiting for it to come back…..

But it wasn't there!

"Blue Butterfly, where did the scared feeling go?" he asked?

"It's disappeared Brian, you used all the strength and happiness inside you to make it so tiny that it just popped out and it's so tiny that you will never be able to find it again!".

"Never?" Brian asked, full of surprise.

"Never and do you know what Brian? Even if you went to a new place and there was a different feeling you know what to do now, don't you?" Blue Butterfly told him.

Brian thought about this for a moment, Blue Butterfly was right, he DID know what to do now! "Oh wow Blue Butterfly, I can make them disappear all on my own now!" he said.

"Exactly, you have learnt a new way to be brave and strong Brian!" Blue Butterfly said!

Brian was so excited that he ran round the garden extra fast! He was so, so happy! His tummy was full of the lovely blue feeling and he felt so much better! He felt happy and brave now!

That afternoon Brian ran around the garden while his mummy was in the house, he knew that she was ok and that he was ok, he could find her if he needed her. So he played and had lots of fun in the garden with Blue Butterfly and his ball.

And as he curled up in his bed that evening Brian knew, that if a funny feeling appeared in his tummy he just needed to:

"Close his eyes and think of something happy and that blue feeling. Then imagine the blue feeling flying all over your body to allow him to feel happy and brave. Then he could just make that blue feeling fly even FASTER so that those magic shooting stars would start flying all around inside him, and as they fly around faster and faster the scared feeling would get smaller and smaller. The smaller it got then the FASTER the shooting stars would move until the scared feeling was really tiny, and as they fly around faster and faster the scared feeling becomes so tiny that you can barely see it and when we count to 5 it just pops out of your belly button, but you wont even feel it! 1…..2……3…….4………5! And just like magic, its GONE!"

And from that day forward Brian never forgot –
that he had all the magic inside him to be happy
and he could just use all the strength and
happiness inside him to make any worries he had
so tiny that he can just POP them out!

Xxx

Other books in this series:

Brian and the Blue Butterfly

Brian and the Magic Night

Brian and the Black Pebble

Brian and the Christmas Wish

Brian and the Shiny Star

Brian and the Naughty Day

Brian and the Funny Feeling

Brian and the Poorly Day

Brian and the Big Black Dog

Brian and the Scary Moment

Nicky lives in Sussex with Brian the Cockapoo where they enjoy daily adventures with friends and family. Nicky started her career by spending 10 years working in the early years sector with 0-5 year olds before lecturing in early years and health and social care to students aged 16 and over. She later retrained as a hypnotherapist and now runs A Step at a Time Hypnotherapy working with children and adults to resolve their personal issues.

The Adventures of Brian books were the development of a dream of wanting to offer parents of young children tools and resources to support their children to manage worries and fears in a non-intrusive way. Having spent a large part of her career reading stories at all speeds and in all voices this collection of storybooks was born.

Each book in the collection covers a different worry which affects children on a day to day basis and uses therapeutic storytelling to support children in resolving these through Brian's daily adventures.

You can find more titles in the Adventures of Brian series by visiting:

www.adventuresofbrian.co.uk

Printed in Great Britain
by Amazon